THE BOY WHO KNEW

While Carlo Acutis was a real person, this is a work of fiction. All names, characters, places, incidents and dialogues in this publication are products of the author's imagination or are used fictitiously. Any resemblance to actual places, events or people, living or dead, is entirely coincidental.

Under the direction of Romain Lizé, President, MAGNIFICAT
Editor, MAGNIFICAT: Isabelle Galmiche
Editors, Ignatius: Vivian Dudro, Gail Gavin
Proofreader: Samuel Wigutow
Layout Cover Designer: Gauthier Delauné
Layout: Text'Oh
Production: Thierry Dubus, Audrey Bord

CORINNA TURNER

FRIENDS IN HIGH PLACES

THE BOY WHO KNEW

—CARLO ACUTIS—

Magnificat • Ignatius

CONTENTS

SATURDAY: DIAGNOSIS DAY

October 3, 2020

You have leukemia.

I keep hearing the doctor's words in my head. I keep seeing the doctor's eyes over his mask, darting from me to my parents. Mum burst into tears. Dad started pounding on the doctor's desk with his fists. I just sat there.

Leukemia. How can I have leukemia? I'm fifteen. Stuff that bad doesn't happen to people my age, right?

But the tiredness ... the bruising ...

You have leukemia.

When we got home from the hospital, Mum started getting ready for the vigil Mass as usual. Dad never comes along these days, but tonight, he started yelling at Mum. "How can you possibly think there is a God if He could let this happen to Daniel? How can you think He is good?"

Mum shouted back, "God is his only hope; can't you see that? Do you want Daniel to die?"

They were still screaming at each other when I slipped out of the house and walked to church. I don't think I've ever come to church on my own before. I felt self-conscious. Any other week, I'd have grabbed the chance to skip Mass. Today, I am angry with God, I suppose ...? But I'm also really, really scared.

And I really wanted to escape the shouting.

Mum never showed up for Mass. I got a text during the First Reading: "Daniel, where are you?" I texted back: "At church." An old lady glared at me over the top of her environmentally unfriendly single-use mask.

I fell asleep during the homily. I'm just so tired all the time. I got glared at again.

Now everyone's gone, and I'm still sitting here. I'm afraid to go home in case Mum and Dad are still arguing. Or in case they want to talk about it all. I feel numb. I haven't even taken my mask off, though I'm alone.

You have leukemia.

Do you want Daniel to die?

Am I going to die? Words from one of the Scripture readings I heard before I nodded off come to mind: *There is no need to worry; but if there is anything you need, pray for it.*

"God, please don't let me die," I whisper.

God doesn't reply. Maybe Dad's right.

Pulling my mask off at last, I shove it into my pocket, my hands shaking.

"God, I'm scared."

Nothing. Well, nothing except that the numbness shatters, and suddenly I really *feel* the fear, which turns my belly into a black hole, cold as a ... morgue?

I bury my face in my hands as the sobs rip from me. *Am I going to die, Lord?*

Distant footsteps from the front of the church.

They pause, then tread briskly along the aisle. Toward me. Oh no.

I wipe my face, desperately trying to stop the gasping, heaving sobs. Snot smears my sleeve. Yuck.

"Hi, Daniel."

Reluctantly, I glance up, my shoulders still shuddering. It's Father Thomas. He's young and kind of cool, sweeping around in his long, black dress—sorry, cassock—without a trace of embarrassment. I wish I had his total lack of self-consciousness.

"Hi, Father." My voice wobbles. *Play it cool, Daniel. Just pretend you're fine and get up and leave.*

"Are you okay?"

"No." I'm shaking my head. What happened to leaving? And then I'm blurting, "I've got leukemia."

His lips part as though I just punched him in the gut. "Oh, Daniel…" He settles into the pew, several feet away because of social distancing. He sits sideways to face me, his eyes narrowed in concern. "Heck, I thought you were going to say you had been bullied or something. That diagnosis is a hard thing to face at any age but especially when you are young. When are you starting treatment? Did they say… what the prognosis is?"

"Prognosis?" I sound like an idiot. Oh, whether I'm going to live or die, he means. "Oh, uh… well, I just got the preliminary test results today. After more tests on Monday morning, the specialists will make a plan, and I'll see them the next Monday, and… well, that's when they'll tell me… you know. They think I'll start treatment almost at once."

"That's good. Just enough time for a novena."

"What?"

He pulls out his wallet and flicks through several business cards before pulling one out. "This is the saint for you. Well, a Blessed, technically. In fact, he's not a Blessed until next Saturday, so I shouldn't really be giving these new cards out yet—but under the circumstances, I think it's okay. Here." He leans over to hand me the little card. "Almost-Blessed Carlo Acutis. He had leukemia when he was fifteen. Best prayer buddy you could have right now. I think there's a novena on his website."

He sees my vague look. "A novena is when you team up with a saint for nine days to pray for something."

"Oh yeah, I remember." I accept the card and slip it into my pocket, though I'm not sure I want it. With the numbness gone, I am starting to feel pretty mad at God. Isn't He supposed to love me? A wire of white-hot rage tightens painfully around my gut, and I scowl toward the tabernacle. Dad's right. How could He let this happen to me? What did I ever do to Him?

"Have you ever made a pot?" asks Father Thomas suddenly. "Or a painting?"

What? "Uh, I make 3D art on my computer. Loads of it."

"Ah, that's right. I knew you were an artist of some kind. Say you created a 3D pot, then. Would anyone have forced you to make it?"

I look at him blankly. "No. I would've done it just because I wanted to."

"Could you, like, virtually smash it?"

"In my program? Sure. More or less." A surge of happiness flows through me at the thought of my state-of-the-art 3D design program… then wilts. What good will it do me if I can't beat this thing?

"Could you take the pieces of your ex-pot and make them into a mosaic that was far more beautiful?"

"If I wanted to."

"And that would be okay? Breaking your pot and remaking it into something better?"

"Of course. It's my pot. I made it, right?"

"And then you could keep your beautiful mosaic forever, right?"

Forever? I may not have a *year*, for all I know. Belatedly, I figure out what he's on about. "Oh, very clever. But I'm not a pot! It's not the same!"

"No, it's not the same," Father Thomas agrees, unperturbed. "We're far more important to God than some 3D pot. Or even a real one. He loves every single hair on our heads—and He knows exactly how many there are."

"Great!" I snap, leaping up from the pew and storming away from his infuriating calm. I yell over my shoulder, "I'll be sure to remember that when they start falling out!"

But I catch his soft words, just before I slip through the door.

"I hope you do."

SUNDAY: DAY 1

October 4, 2020

I close my bedroom door and start to flop onto my bed, then let myself down more carefully. Seems like every little thing bruises me these days. Arnie creeps onto my lap, purring. Dad had gone down to the pub before I got back last night, and Mum's eyes were all red. My little sister, Clare, just stood and stared at me, chewing at her thumb, which was too weird because she usually never shuts up. What did they tell her?

I said I wasn't hungry and went straight to bed. I wasn't lying; I don't think I could've eaten a thing.

Now it's Sunday morning, and after sneaking a quick bowl of cereal in the kitchen, I've returned to my room to hide out. Sooner or later, Mum and Dad will want to "talk about things," and I'm dreading it.

"Try not to think about it too much," the doctor told me. "When we've got all the tests and have planned the treatment, we'll have a much better idea what's what."

Try not to think about it. I'd like to see him try not to think about it!

I shift Arnie back onto the bed, then drag myself up. I walk over to my computer and turn it on, then open an internet browser. I type in "acute leukemia, ALL type." Open an article.

Click straight through to "What's the outlook?"

My eyes pick out phrases: "Children aged between one year and ten years have the best outlook." Ten? I'm fifteen! I keep reading.

"In those aged fourteen or younger, more than nine in ten will survive leukemia for five years or longer after diagnosis."

I stare at that, my stomach churning. I'm fifteen, not fourteen. And if you told me I had a nine-out-of-ten chance of winning something, I'd normally be thrilled. But a one-in-ten chance of *dying* seems… huge. And even the nine-out-of-ten chance is for living only five years.

I hit the X to close the web page and wrap my arms around myself, shivering. I can't look at this anymore. My hand brushes something in my jeans pocket, and I pull out the card Father Thomas gave me. Huh, I thought he said it was a saint card. But a cheerful boy my age, dressed in modern clothes, stares up at me from a color photo. This is a saint? Well, a Blessed, he said. That's a junior saint, right?

I read the simple text: "Blessed Carlo Acutis, pray for us."

Glad of the distraction, I open a new browser and type in the strange name, then click on the first result.

"Born 1991 in England," I read. Born 1991? Seriously? That's so recent. I thought you had to be dead hundreds of years to be a saint, even a junior one.

Hang on. If he was only born in 1991, how can he be a saint already? I read on quickly. "Diagnosed with leukemia in 2006"—yeah, that's what Father said—"and died 2006." What? No way! I launch the card across the room, making it tap against the far wall and fall to the ground with a papery sigh. Father Thomas thinks I want to read about a kid with leukemia who *died*? Is he nuts?

But the web page is open in front of me, and I can't help

scrolling down.

He was born in London—huh, like me—because his parents were there on business, but—unlike me—they soon moved back to Italy, where he grew up as an only child. Good student, special kid, blah blah blah, everybody liked him, blah blah blah. Parents not practicing, but little Carlo was so holy—never passing a church without wanting to go in and "say hello to Jesus"—that it brought his mum back to the faith, then his dad. Yeah, fine, very nice. Come on, I want to know about his disease.

I read: "Carlo often said, 'I will die young.'" Weird. He *knew*? How? Did the Holy Spirit tell him? Wait, here are the details. "Diagnosed early October... acute leukemia... died..."—wait, just *one week* later?

Waves of coldness wash over me. My head buzzes in terror. Nausea chokes my throat.

Oh yeah, Father Thomas, I'm so comforted!

I reach out to close the web page, but my eye catches a word on the menu: *Novena.*

Just enough time for a novena.

God is Daniel's only hope!

Is that true?

I click the button and skim through an opening prayer inattentively. No, if I'm doing this, I suppose I should do it properly. I'm not sure that I want to, though. Dad would be disgusted, the way he carried on last night. Never mind; he'll never know. I make myself read the opening prayer properly, and when it finishes with "Ask the grace which you seek," I whisper, "Let me live. Please!"

Then comes the First Day Meditation, which starts with something Carlo said himself: "Not me, but God." From what I've just read, God was the focus of Carlo's life, even when he was just a little kid.

My heart sinks. What's this got to do with me? Carlo was so holy. I'm not holy like that. I carry on reading. The meditation talks about setting aside unimportant things, seeking heavenly things, and despising that which is transient. Like… life? My stomach chills even more. Is there any point in asking this dead boy to be—what did Father Thomas call it?—my prayer buddy?

God is Daniel's only hope!

This dead boy who was so holy he knew his own future. Huh. I recite the Our Fathers, Hail Marys, and Glory Bes, speaking clearly.

Blessed Carlo, I'm not holy like you. But if you're not dead and rotted and… gone… the way Dad thinks, I could really use your help. Please?

MONDAY: DAY 2

October 5, 2020

I bend my head and pretend to be busy on my phone, trying to tune out the noise of the cafeteria. Mum wanted me to stay at home today, but I persuaded her to drop me at school after we were done at the hospital. But I really don't want to talk to my friends. I can't bear anyone to know about this until… until I know. I gave my classmates some vague excuse for arriving late.

I feel exhausted already. I bet I'm going to crash when I get home. Maybe I should do my novena now. I'm still a bit unsure about it, but I've started it, so I want to finish it. Eight days until Prognosis Day.

Quickly, I find the web page. In my head, I recite the opening prayer again, adding my request: *Don't let me die. Please?* And scroll down to the meditation for Day 2. Oh dear. Today's quote from almost-Blessed Carlo is just as holy as the first one. "Always to be united with Jesus—that is my life's program." He's making me feel kind of guilty. I mean, I think I believe. I've always gone to church with Mum without complaining—at least not much. Dad told me I didn't have to get confirmed if I didn't want to, but I decided I did. But how seriously do I really take my faith from day to day? I go to Mass on Sunday, but since the confirmation course finished, that's it.

Silently, I say the rest of the prayers, concentrating as well as I can in this noisy place. Then I click on "Biography" and start reading more attentively than I did yesterday. Soon I'm puzzled, though: Carlo sounds so ordinary! He liked video games and European football, like me. And joking and laughing. And kites, cartoons, and action films. He even loved Pokémon characters! A saint who likes Pokémon? I guess Pokémon was cool back then, but it's weird.

Hey, he loved animals, too! He had two cats, four dogs, and loads of goldfish, the lucky thing. I would love a dog, but Mum's very allergic. I have Arnie, but only on condition that I clean the litter tray myself, vacuum the carpets for Mum an extra time each week, and never let him in Mum and Dad's room or Mum's study—because she's mildly allergic to cats too. Arnie was a rescue, and he's getting quite old, so he spends most of his time sleeping on my bed and less time shedding fur around the house.

The novena website calls Carlo a computer geek. He wrote computer programs and designed websites. Apparently he may be patron saint of the internet one day! His interests were a bit more technical than what I get up to; I like the arty stuff more. But he did video editing and edited comics! I've done some of that.

It's cool having so much in common with an almost-Blessed. But as I read on, I begin to notice the differences too. He loved computer games, but… what? He allowed himself to play for only one hour a week! He thought there were so many better things he could be doing. Huh. I think of all the hours I spend messing around in my 3D design program. But I'm creating art, right? Beautiful things. Not the same, right? Hmm.

A scuffle breaks out across the cafeteria—Marle the bully

going after Lame Richard again. Staff descend, yelling at everyone to get back to their class tables at once: "No mixing. Masks on. How many times do we have to tell you?" I go back to my phone.

Whoa, seriously? Carlo went to Mass *every day*! Why would you even do that? He turned down a holiday to Jerusalem on one occasion, saying, "If Jesus remains with us always, wherever there is a consecrated Host, what need is there to make a pilgrimage to visit the places where Jesus lived two thousand years ago?"

Huh, there's another quote from him: "If we get in front of the sun, we get suntans… but when we get in front of Jesus in the Eucharist, we become saints."

I frown at the text on the screen. Carlo's breaking my brain, seriously. The way he's so ordinary and holy all at once. The way he talks about "us" becoming saints. I mean, that's not just him, right? That's… me and him. *Me*? That's crazy.

Carlo believed, "The Eucharist is my highway to heaven!"

I stare at my phone until Razim says, "Hey, Daniel, you okay?"

"Huh?" I look around and crank a smile onto my face, giving a thumbs-up a second later as I remember I'm wearing my mask. "Yeah, fine." I turn back to my phone quickly, not wanting to talk.

I feel Raz's eyes on me for a moment or two, then he starts talking to someone else. I reread the paragraph I just read. Daily Eucharist to get to heaven is fine for Carlo, but I don't need that. Me, I'm going to live. That's why I'm doing this novena, right?

I mean to tap away from the article, but I find myself reading on. Apparently Carlo received his First Holy Communion early, at his own request. A bishop—no, not just a bishop, but the pope's former personal secretary—had to confirm that he was mature enough. The bishop even suggested that the ceremony take place somewhere peaceful, without the distractions of a big party. So, seven-year-old Carlo walked into a silent monastery under a doorway that said "God is enough" to receive for the first time. Huh.

I can't help thinking of my First Holy Communion. Dad was there; he still came to church occasionally back then. But the main thing I remember is the party afterward—and my new Xbox. I bite my lip and read more of Carlo's words.

"Conversion is none other than stopping looking downwards and starting to look upwards. You just have to move your eyes."

Move your eyes? That's how you can become holy? You just shift your gaze? There's got to be more to it than that.

Right?

TUESDAY: DAY 3

October 6, 2020

I was so tired when I got home yesterday, but I want to be here at school, to keep things normal. Mum and Dad both work from home. Every time Mum looks at me, her eyes fill with tears. And Dad keeps sniping at her about God. I just wish he'd stop. I know he hasn't practiced his faith for years, but he didn't used to go on about it.

I doubt I'm going to feel any better when I get home today, so as soon as I've eaten my lunch, I pull out my phone and open the novena page.

Hey, today's quote from Carlo is a bit more on my level: "Continuously ask your guardian angel for help. Your guardian angel has to become your best friend." That's a bit more doable, right? "Give me the grace to live righteously, as my guardian angel desires," says the meditation. *As my guardian angel desires.* I rub my fingertip over a bruise on the back of my hand, then tug my sleeve down to hide it. I've never really thought about my guardian angel as having *desires* before, like a person. But aren't angels individuals, kind of, the same way people are?

And my guardian angel desires me to be righteous? Yeah, I guess it—he?—does. That's, like, his whole purpose in life, right? Not to help me be physically safe but to help me be spiritually safe. I remember Father Thomas saying that during confirmation class.

That's a shame. I could use some physical help right now.

I say the novena prayers, then go back to the article about almost-Blessed Carlo. Carlo even made a website where people could find which saints in heaven were suited to be their friends. An "internet genius," one guy called him.

Well, getting to know one saintly friend is enough for me. Carlo's still giving me whiplash. Apparently he was really kind to everyone—especially anyone who wasn't fitting in at school or who had disabilities. He defended them against bullies. Yet he was really popular, despite inviting his friends to church stuff all the time and even defending his pro-life views in class! He treated girls with an old-fashioned purity that amazed his friends and should have got him laughed out of school—but it didn't, because he had such… *conviction*. He had absolutely no interest in conforming: "All people are born as originals, but many die as photocopies."

I glance around the cafeteria. Is that what we're all doing? Trying to turn ourselves into photocopies?

"Why do people worry so much about their physical beauty but don't worry about the beauty of their souls?" Carlo would say.

The ugly bruise on my hand is showing again. I'm about to tug my sleeve down again despite Carlo's words, when a scuffle breaks out.

"No, give it back!" Lame Richard's voice, high and distressed. "I'll get sick if I don't wear it! Mum said!"

I glance around the cafeteria. No staff.

"Go on, kiss my trainers while you're down there, and I'll let you up. Might even give your mask back—after I use it to wipe my nose, of course!" Marle's voice carries across the cafeteria, and a lot of people laugh; some climb up on tables to see better.

Anger makes me properly hot for the first time since I got the diagnosis. Lame Richard is a special-needs student, and everyone knows he's immunocompromised. Taking his mask and trying to make him kiss dirty trainers?

Carlo, help me! I just can't sit here today and—

I get to my feet and storm up the aisle, ignoring my friends' shouts of dismay. Marle is seventeen and, like, twice my size. But what does it matter, seeing as I may be going to die anyway?

"Get off him!" I shove Marle away, but when I reach to help Richard up, Marle grabs my wrist, squeezing hard.

"He's staying down there, you cocky little snot-rag!"

"No. He's not!" My nose comes up only to Marle's collarbone, but I refuse to back down.

Marle is not used to someone standing up to him, and a flicker of uncertainty goes through his eyes. Ha! Coward.

"Everyone, back to your class tables! *How many times do we have to tell you?*"

Marle lets go of my wrist, chucks the mask at Richard, and slips in among his classmates. I reach toward Lame Richard again, then think better of it. Immunocompromised—like me. But as he lurches to his feet, his gaze is fixed on my wrist, where a dark bruise is already forming. Self-consciously, I pull my sleeve down, give him an awkward thumbs-up in place of a grin he won't see behind my mask, and head for the door. If I go back to my table, my friends will be all over me.

I settle in the empty classroom and go back to reading.

"What is the point of winning a thousand battles if we can't win the battle with ourselves?" says Carlo.

Huh. I still check that my sleeves are down before the rest of the class joins me. It's not vanity, right? I just don't want them to know yet.

"What's up, man? You gone crazy?" asks Razim as he drops my bag beside me and slaps me on the back, making all my bruises twinge. "Taking on Marle all by yourself!" His gaze wobbles between admiration and concern as he stares at me.

I mumble something about being fed up with Marle picking on Richard, and—thank God—the teacher enters before Raz can say any more.

When I reach home, I can see Mum and Dad in the front room, yelling and gesticulating, so I trudge straight past the house and on to church. Settle into a back pew. I should pray. But I can't find the words. And I'm so, so tired…

Buzz.

I wake with a jolt and straighten, my neck aching. My backside too. Pews aren't meant for sleeping in. I check my phone. I've been asleep forty-five minutes. A text from Mum just arrived: "Where are you? Are you OK?"

I want to text back: *I was fine until I got home and saw you two at it again. It's bad enough maybe-dying without your parents splitting up over it.*

But I don't. I hope my guardian angel is proud of me.

WEDNESDAY: DAY 4

October 7, 2020

"I'm not staying here with you two all day. Just *forget it*!" I slam the front door and leg it down the street. I'm barely around the corner before I have to stop and lean against the wall, gasping for breath.

Guess that guardian angel of mine won't be so proud of me this morning. But what good is it going to do, my sitting around at home?

"Are you okay, Daniel?" Razim asks me at break time. "You look so… you're really acting… kind of weird at the moment."

"I'm fine, Razim. Really." Then I feel bad. Because, really, I just lied to him, right? "Well, my parents are fighting a lot. It's getting me down." That's half the truth, at least.

At lunch I keep my head down and do my novena. The meditation has a long quote today: "Our soul is like a hot-air balloon. If by chance there is a mortal sin, the soul falls to the ground. Confession is like the fire underneath the balloon enabling the soul to rise again.… It is important to go to confession often."

I read it twice, then picture my soul rising up and down like a hot-air balloon as I heedlessly lob lead weights into the basket while a Jesus figure who looks rather like Father Thomas chucks them out again, the whole time trying to keep a Holy Spirit burner blazing away. I guess it's a pretty good metaphor.

I haven't been to confession since Lent. Maybe I should go. I hate going to confession, though, even to Father Thomas. Do I really need to?

But the sound of a slamming door echoes in my mind as I do the novena prayers. And when I switch to the article, I read Carlo's words: "In order to rise to God, the soul must shed even its smallest weights."

I ring the rectory doorbell, feeling super awkward. This is stupid. He's probably not even in. But I couldn't go straight home after school. Mum and Dad were fighting *again*. And the church is full of little masked and mantilla-ed old ladies praying a Rosary.

Father Thomas opens the door and smiles. "Oh, hi, Daniel. Do you want to come in?"

I nod, so he steps back. After I've used his hand sanitizer, he leads me to the front room with the wide windows, where I often see him talking with parishioners. He waves to the sofa, then converts the invitation to a "stop" gesture. "Hold up, I'll change the cover."

He pulls the throw off the sofa and carries it away. I hear him using the hand sanitizer in the hall and opening a cupboard. A moment later he's back with a clean, neatly folded throw.

He shakes it out and tosses it over the couch. "There."

Yeah, I'm immunocompromised now. Maybe that's why Mum doesn't want me in school. A worm of guilt stirs in my belly as I remember the way I yelled at her earlier.

I sit on the sofa, and Father Thomas takes the armchair on the other side of the room, so there's plenty of air between us.

"I'm sorry I snapped at you the other day," I mumble.

He dismisses this with a flick of his hand. "How are you?"

"Fine, I guess. I mean, I was so mad at you for being so calm about it. Felt like you didn't care. But Mum practically bursts into tears every time she looks at me, though she keeps telling me how it's all going to be fine, and Dad won't stop giving her a hard time, and my sister just stares at me as if she's afraid I'm going to go *poof* and vanish, so… so actually, it's really nice to sit here with someone who's matter-of-fact about it."

Father Thomas smiles, white teeth gleaming against his dark skin. "I care, Daniel. You know that, right? But, you're still here; you're still you. How *should* I treat you?"

After a moment, I smile back at him. His words make me feel better. Yeah, he does care. He's just not getting hysterical about it, and boy, do I need some of that right now!

"How are your parents taking this?"

My shoulders hunch. "They're just fighting all the time. About how God let this happen to me."

"Oh." Father Thomas sighs. "I'm sorry to hear that. How do you feel?"

"Well, there is some truth in your pot metaphor, I suppose. Your *lame* pot metaphor," I add—then regret being mean. "Uh, I'm doing the novena. At first, I was so mad when I looked up Carlo. I mean, why'd you give me a saint who *died*? But, uh, I've been enjoying reading about him, actually."

Father Thomas shrugs. "Same age, same disease. Sue me for hoping the two of you would get along. By the way, I wanted to ask, which type of leukemia do you have? ALL or AML?"

Has he been doing his research? "ALL."

He nods. "Good. Almost-Blessed Carlo had the other type. It's far deadlier."

He did? A slight knot untwists in my gut. But the guilt is still lodged there.

"You know," he goes on, "Carlo used to make a special point of helping kids whose parents were having marital difficulties. He'd invite those kids home and befriend them. Why not add your mum and dad to your novena? Don't get mad at me for saying this, but in some ways, this is even harder for them."

Harder for them? Is it? I file that away to think about later and gather my resolve. I mean, different type or not, what if I just get worse *really* fast, like Carlo did?

"Father? Could I, um..."—*Carlo, help!*—"could I . . . do you think I could... confess?"

A big smile spreads over his face. "You certainly may."

THURSDAY: DAY 5

October 8, 2020

"Daniel, is that you? You okay?"

I turn from closing the front door. "Yes, Mum."

I came straight home from school today because I didn't want to worry her again. I keep thinking about what Father Thomas told me yesterday, after I confessed to yelling at her.

Do you know what almost the last words Carlo spoke were? He couldn't sleep because of the pain, and a nurse asked him if he'd like her to wake his mother so she could keep him company. But he said to let her sleep because "she is very tired as well, and she will only worry even more."

Carlo was lying there, dying—and he knew he was dying—but he cared more about his mother's comfort than his own. It's like his quote in the novena today: "Sadness is looking at ourselves; happiness is looking toward God." Carlo was so *happy*. That's what people who knew him say. And he found God in others, right?

I'm really trying to be more patient with Mum, anyway.

She comes out to the hall. "Father Thomas phoned a few minutes ago. Wanted you to ring him as soon as you got home. But if you need to rest first..."

"No, I'm fine. In fact"—ugh, her eyes are getting that look

again—"I . . . uh, I think I'll just stroll along there. I'd like some fresh air."

Soon I'm leaning against the rectory doorway as I ring the bell, breathing hard. I can't believe how exhausted I feel, especially since I didn't even have to walk to school this morning because Razim's dad gave us a lift. I must be getting worse.

Father Thomas opens the door. "Oh, Daniel! You didn't need to come all the way over here."

"I felt like a walk."

He leads the way to the front room. I stand, legs shaking, while he changes the throw again. Then I sink down on the sofa, still trying to catch my breath.

"Do you want a drink? You look shattered. Juice, coffee?"

"Uh, juice? Thanks."

He heads off to get it. What does he want to talk to me about?

I'm lying in a hospital bed, tubes coming from my arms. Machines beep. Fear rises inside me as I look around.

But my friend is sitting by my bed. He smiles, a big, radiant smile that lights up the room. The light is beautiful. "I've got your back, Daniel."

I relax into the pillows, my fear easing. Carlo murmurs something else, softly. Prayers. I'm so relaxed, I don't feel I need to strain to hear, so I just catch snippets.

". . . for they loved not their lives even unto death . . ."

"Rejoice, then, O heaven and you that dwell therein."

"The Lord fed us with finest wheat."

"Give eternal rest to the dead: bring the whole Church together in heaven."

Huh? I open my eyes. No Carlo. No hospital. Father Thomas stands facing a crucifix in the corner, holding a leather-bound book in his hand, reciting some sort of prayer. How long have I been asleep? When I sit up, a clean-smelling blanket slides down off me.

Father Thomas crosses himself and closes the book, then turns around. "Ah, Daniel."

My cheeks burn. "I'm really sorry. I didn't mean to fall asleep!"

"It's fine. You've had a nap, and I've done my prayers. Win-win." He gestures to a glass beside me and takes his well-distanced armchair again.

I pick up the juice and drink thirstily. Sugar, energy: that's what I need.

"Well, Daniel, I'll make this quick because you'd better get home before your parents worry. You know I said Carlo Acutis is being beatified—made a Blessed—this Saturday?"

I nod over the top of my glass.

"Well, because he was born in the UK, we were asked to send a representative to Assisi for the ceremony. The bishops chose a young man with leukemia to go. But... uh, well, he can't go, unexpectedly, so they sent an email around yesterday asking for other candidates. I put your name forward. And, well, they chose you."

I accidentally spit the last bit of juice back into the glass. "What? Hang on. Are you saying—"

"That you're going to Assisi for the beatification? Yes, I am."

"Please, Mum! I'm well enough!"

Father Thomas insisted on driving me home, even though it's only a few blocks, and he's just asked my parents about the trip.

"You can't go on your own! You're too young!"

Helplessly, I look at Father Thomas, who nods. "The original representative was old enough to travel unaccompanied without any concerns. But the bishops are happy to send one other person with Daniel because of his age."

"So you can come with me, Mum! Just think, Assisi! Saint Francis!"

Mum looks agonized. "Leaving *tomorrow*? I can't, Daniel. I'm in the middle of something big. And especially if I'm going to have to take lots of time—" She breaks off. "I'd *love* to come, but I can't. I'm really sorry."

"Then… Dad can come?" I look at him, my heart sinking. Dad? Come to a major religious thing? Right at the moment?

He won't meet my gaze. He simply shakes his head. "I can't take time off either."

I just don't believe it! Italy, Assisi, Carlo's big day!

I want to thump the wall, but I'd bruise myself worse than what Marle did to my wrist two days ago. Father Thomas looks upset, dismayed he's gotten my hopes up, I guess. Hang on…

"Father Thomas, can you come with me?"

"Me? Uh, I really don't think…" I stare at him, pleading, and he trails off. He then holds up a finger in a "give me a minute" gesture, looking like a man who's mentally juggling with an overflowing schedule. I can hardly breathe.

"Um… I suppose I *could* fly out with you as scheduled tomorrow evening. I could get someone to cover the Saturday Masses. But I'll never find cover for the Sunday Masses, so we'd have to catch a flight back on Saturday evening. You wouldn't see much of Assisi."

"I don't care! I'd still make the beatification, right? Mum, Dad, can I go?" I turn my pleading gaze on them.

Mum looks from me to Father Thomas. "Well… I suppose so."

Dad glowers, though, and says nothing.

"Dad!" I appeal. "I've never been to Italy! I've barely been anywhere!"

And this might be my only chance hangs in the air unsaid, but I can tell Dad hears it. He glowers at Father Thomas even harder. "Fine. But he gets his own room, so… so he can rest whenever he needs to!"

Father Thomas' eyebrows draw together, just slightly—or maybe I'm imagining it, because he speaks lightly enough. "Goes without saying. Can you sign the consent form as soon as the diocese emails it over?" He glances at me. "You take it easy tomorrow, okay? I'll email you the time we need to depart when I've worked it out."

I nod, my heart pounding. I don't believe it.

I'm going to Assisi!

I'll actually be at Carlo's beatification!

FRIDAY: DAY 6

October 9, 2020

I allow Mum to talk me out of going to school today. I need to pack, and I don't want to be so tired that she decides not to let me travel after all. And I don't think I can sit beside Razim all day and not spill the beans. And then I'd have to tell him everything.

I do insist on walking down to the shopping street to get some things for the trip. I did my novena, first thing, and I think about it as I walk, because the meditation is troubling me. Today the quote from Carlo was this: "The only thing we have to ask God for, in prayer, is the desire to be holy." But that's not what I've been asking for, is it?

The meditation talks about how Carlo always asked God for "what is essential." "Give me the grace of a deep desire for heaven"—those are the words I prayed earlier. Did I mean them?

By the time I reach the pharmacy, I'm too tired to think about it anymore. I don't even remember to put my mask on until I'm reaching for the sanitizer. Total brain fog. I locate earplugs, an eye mask, and a neck pillow as fast as I can, adding a pack of disposable surgical masks as well. I like my custom fabric ones with my own art designs printed on them, but Mum says

I should wear a hospital-grade one on the plane for maximum protection.

I grab a few depressingly healthy snacks from beside the cash register as well. That will have to do. I've got to go home and rest. A taxi is coming at four o'clock to take me and Father Thomas to the airport.

I'm getting breathless again as I walk back down the busy shopping street. My legs wobble under me. Ugh, it's no good; I can't keep going. I sit down hastily on a bench and put my head between my knees. Why did I come out? I've *got* to be okay for tonight! But it's only a short walk from home. I'm getting worse, must be.

A bad smell reaches my nose, and a shadow moves beside me.

"Hey, kid, you okay?"

I look around. It's the homeless guy who often sits begging nearby. He disappeared during lockdown, and now he's back. "Yeah, I'm just a bit tired."

"You sure?" Under his overgrown hair, his worn face is drawn with worry. "Everything okay at home, kid?" His eyes are on my wrist, where Marle's handprint stands out on my pale skin in brutal black and blue.

I sit up and pull my sleeve down. "Yeah, honestly. That's not what it looks like. Well, it is, but it's not what you think. I've got leukemia." I surprise myself, saying it, just like that.

His face crumples up in dismay. "Sheesh, it's a rare day when I meet someone who's got it worse than me. Reminds me to be grateful for my blessings, that does."

Which are few enough, by the look of him. I force myself not to think about his stench and glance around. "I'm going to go in the coffee shop and rest for a few minutes. Do you want to come and have something too?"

Surprise flits across his face, then he smiles. "That'd be great."

We're installed in a booth, sitting the usual distance apart, and I'm trying harder than ever to ignore his suffocating body odor as he tucks into a sandwich. I guess he can't help it. He doesn't have a house to shower in. I sip a coffee, hoping the caffeine will give me the energy to get home and walk into the house looking healthy enough to travel.

The guy keeps shooting me looks as he eats, though.

"What?" I ask eventually. Not angrily. Just asking.

He shrugs. "Oh, kids your age are often quicker to kick a bottle at a fellow than buy him a meal. And you've never really looked at me before."

He recognizes me? My cheeks burn. I guess he would. I've lived here since I was born, and he's been sitting there for years, off and on.

"Well, uh..." I take a sip of coffee to hide my confusion. "Well, I kind of... made a new friend recently. And, uh, he spent loads of time volunteering at an orphanage, and with the elderly, and in a soup kitchen too. Makes me feel I really don't... you know, pull my weight."

He grins, showing stained teeth. "Sounds like a real nice guy. You're lucky to have a mate like that."

"Yeah. I'm starting to think I am."

A swish of black outside draws my eyes. Father Thomas is passing—on his way back from the pharmacy too? I raise a hand and wave, catching his attention. He turns into the coffee shop, slides into our booth, and settles at an appropriate distance. "Hi, Daniel. Hi, Greg."

Greg. Heat rises in my cheeks.

I never even asked him his name—or told him mine!

I have a sudden, crystal-clear image in my mind of Carlo sitting beside me, rolling his eyes.

"I've got to sit down for a minute."

Father Thomas is walking home with me, since it's on his way, but we're only halfway there when I sink down on a low wall.

"Are you okay, Daniel?"

"Fine. Just tired. Please don't mention this to my mum. This Assisi trip is the one good thing about having cancer." Well, the trip and learning about Carlo. The more I find out about him, the more hopeful he makes me feel. It's as if I'm opening the door to a dark, empty room inside me, and the more I open the door, the more light streams in, revealing beautiful things I didn't know were there.

Father Thomas looks worried, though.

"I'll rest all afternoon. I promise!"

"All right, all right. Calm down."

I sit in silence for a few moments. Carlo makes me feel braver, but still…

"Father Thomas? Do you think I'm going to die?" Ugh, why am I asking him? He's not a doctor.

He cocks his head slightly. "Of course you are." He raises an eyebrow. "We all do, you know."

"Ugh, *Father*!" I buffet his arm with my fist. Oops! I barely touched him, but I'm going to have bruises. "That's not funny!"

He grins, making me lose my indignation and burst out laughing.

But it soon tails off. I don't mean to say it, but I just blurt out: "Father, I'm really scared."

He loses the smile at once. Nods. "Yeah. That's totally natural, okay? But do you know what Carlo said when he heard his diagnosis?"

I've read the words several times in the last few days, so I recite them: "'I am happy to die because I have lived my life without wasting a minute on those things which do not please God.' But *I* haven't, Father Thomas!"

"But you're not dead yet, are you? You may live years, even decades. And even if you've got only months, or weeks, or a few days, well, that doesn't stop you from using the time well, does it? Many people think that's why Carlo was such a whirlwind of life and activity and kindness and generosity—because he knew he hadn't long, and he didn't want to waste a moment. He really wasn't so different from you, Daniel. Just a normal boy who knew where his priorities lay."

Priorities. Where do my priorities lie? I thought I knew last week. My 3D art. My friends. My cat, even.

Now I'm not so sure.

SATURDAY: DAY 7

October 10, 2020

After a tasty continental breakfast at the monastery guesthouse where we arrived late last night—and two cups of superstrong Italian coffee to get me going—we head for the front door. There I find an honest-to-God mobility scooter waiting. You've got to be kidding me! Father Thomas bears my embarrassed fuming, telling me bluntly that I can choose to use it and we'll probably be able to see several of the sites, or I can refuse and we'll probably see only the main basilica—the way he assumed our visit would go before he had this mortifying idea.

I climb on. It's actually surprisingly speedy and rather fun. Father Thomas jogs along after me, grinning at my glee. I bet Carlo would've had fun on this thing too! Razim, as well, if he could be persuaded to give it a chance.

We go to the mighty Basilica of Saint Mary of the Angels first. Inside I'm astonished to find a tiny, complete chapel–the Portiuncula–one of the run-down churches Saint Francis restored, Father Thomas informs me, and near which he died. There aren't many people here yet, and Father Thomas leaves me to pray in the chapel alone. Peace fills me as I sit and soak in the calm of the simple, ancient interior.

Eventually I get out my phone and do my novena. "The

Virgin Mary is the only Woman in my life" is the quote from Carlo. Yeah, he used to say his Rosary every day, without fail. Even during the last few days of his life, in the hospital, he recited it with his family. I gaze up at the old painting of the Annunciation over the altar, showing Mary calmly listening to the Angel Gabriel as he drops the bombshell that will upend her life—and even endanger it. She could've been stoned to death for being with child while she was yet unmarried, I remember Father Thomas saying.

When the doctors told Carlo he was dying, he listened just as calmly. He merely looked around himself and told his mother, "I would like to leave this hospital, but I know I will not do so alive. I will give you signs, though, that I am with God."

What will *I* do on Monday, if the prognosis is bad? Cry? Rage? Turn against God, like Dad? Accept it, with peace in my heart, like Carlo? Like Mary?

Sitting here now, enfolded in this peace, for the first time I almost believe that I might be able to do that, after all—receive the news calmly, even if it is not what I want to hear. I try to memorize the feeling, bottle some carefully in my heart for later use.

When Father Thomas comes back, he leads me to the Chapel of the Renunciation. On this spot, Saint Francis famously took off all his clothes and renounced his father's possessions, walking away stark naked. This is where Carlo has been reburied, now that he's—almost—a Blessed.

The new tomb is built to look as if it were levitating, with light radiating all around it. It's breathtaking, but I hardly notice, because—

I fall to my knees, staring, my mouth dry with shock and awe.

I can see *inside* the tomb. A side panel has been replaced with glass, and Carlo is lying on the other side of it, dressed in jeans and a casual sports top. As Father Thomas kneels down beside me, he murmurs, "There were rumors he was incorrupt, but nothing was officially confirmed. Even if they've added some wax and stuff… wow."

Wow, indeed. Carlo's face, skin, hands look perfect, his hair, everything. No trace of decomposition at all. Dead? He just looks as if he were asleep.

But he's been buried for fourteen years, right? He should've been a skeleton with a bit of hair after just one year—that's what they say on that crime investigators program Razim watches. But his body seems intact.

I reach out hesitantly and lay my hand on the glass. The physical part of Carlo is right here, so solidly real… the closeness makes my head spin. For a while I can do nothing but stare at him, at every flawless detail. His face is relaxed, wearing an expression of peaceful rest. He looks so gentle.

Eventually I manage to close my eyes and silently speak to him about the things that are weighing on me. *Carlo, please pray for my parents. You've made me feel so much better about everything; please help them too.* I've been adding them to my novena intention, the way Father Thomas suggested, but it feels as if praying for them right here is extra special.

A deep, deep sense of welcome enfolds me, as if I'm chilling with a best friend who's really pleased to see me. Tears spill from my eyes; I can't help it. I don't want to leave. I really don't.

Of course, finally, I have to tear myself away.

"So, does that mean he's definitely a saint?" I demand of Father Thomas, as soon as I've got my breathing back under control and I'm feeling slightly less as if I've been hit over the head with a cudgel.

He smiles as he strides alongside the mobility scooter. "Actually, no. If they haven't announced he's properly incorrupt, then they've almost certainly used some wax or something on his face to make him fully, uh, presentable. Anyway, a significant level of incorruption *is* highly indicative of holiness, but only outright miracles are considered concrete evidence for sainthood. Incorruption is often only partial, or delayed decomposition only, and people are concerned that there might be some obscure scientific explanation. So, an incorrupt body is not considered hard proof of being a saint. Perhaps it's overcaution, but that's to be preferred in such matters, wouldn't you say? Canonization is about certainty, not probability."

It's not hard proof? I frown. The bar for sainthood is definitely high, then. Certainty, not probability, huh? That's good, I suppose. But it was amazing to see Carlo like that. I've really, totally met him now!

We head down the hill to see the San Damiano Chapel and pray before the famous painted crucifix—even I've heard of the miraculous San Damiano crucifix, from which Saint Francis heard the voice of God calling him! Although the church is as crowded as social distancing will allow, it has the same simple beauty as the Portiuncula, and I catch a fleeting breath of that peace during a lull in the noise. I'm particularly stoked to see the convent afterward, because it's the site of one of the Eucharistic miracles Carlo documented.

"Can you believe he started dragging his parents all over the world at the age of eleven, to see all the places where Eucharistic miracles happened?" I say to Father Thomas as we head inside. "He took loads of photos! And then he made a website and a traveling display to share the miracles with everyone else when he was fourteen. I can't even imagine organizing something like that!"

This is the place where Saint Clare of Assisi—my little sister's patron saint—drove off a Saracen army simply by showing them the Blessed Sacrament. Well, I suppose Jesus in the Holy Eucharist drove them off. But it was quite inexplicable, anyway, that a marauding army would leave all those unarmed nuns and flee.

A rest at a café—yeah, I sleep for twenty minutes, slumped over my scooter, then drink more strong Italian coffee—and we head to the main Basilica of Saint Francis of Assisi, where the beatification will take place later. In a nearby building, we eat lunch with the cardinal who's going to do the actual beatifying and some of the other representatives. Most of them speak different languages from each other, so there's a lot of nodding and smiling. Afterward, Father Thomas takes me to a neighboring convent, where some kind nuns let me lie down on a bed and sleep for an hour. By that point I'm too tired to object, scooter or no scooter.

I get up in time for a quick look around the huge church. Then it's the big event itself.

The Mass and the beatification ceremony seem a bit anticlimactic. Not many people are here, for one thing, because of the virus. But at least there are some. At one point a little procession comes up the aisle—two men in robes carrying something elaborate, followed by a man and a woman in normal clothes. Father Thomas whispers to me that the ornate object is called a reliquary, and it contains Carlo's intact heart! And the man and the woman—now being embraced by the cardinal—are Carlo's mother and father. Wow. How must they be feeling today?

Since the ceremony is all in Latin or Italian—I'm not sure which—I don't understand much. Still, we receive Jesus at Communion.

I was planning to walk up to Communion by myself, leaving the scooter in the wide-spaced pew—I'm not a complete invalid. Yet. But the priests come around to each member of the congregation in turn. Carlo used to say, "The more we receive the Eucharist, the more we become similar to Jesus and already on this earth we foretaste heaven." After my experience of peace this morning, that's something I'm determined to take more seriously from now on.

A big image of Carlo was unveiled at the front of the church halfway through, and everyone clapped. I keep looking at it, remembering the peace I felt as I prayed this morning. Just one week ago, I would have thought it impossible that I could ever feel like that. How would I be feeling now, without my strange, new, dead, not-dead friend? Two days to Prognosis Day. I should be terrified, depressed, angry, filled with hate for the universe, but I'm not. Yeah, I'm scared, but I feel hope for the future too—in a strange way, more hope than I've felt, ever. Hope wasn't really part of my life before.

"Thank you, Carlo," I whisper before we leave.

Into a taxi. I fall asleep at once, and the next thing I know, it's the better part of two hours later, night has fallen, and we're pulling up outside the Basilica of Saint Francis in Siena. Father Thomas was really smart—we flew into Perugia last night, close to Assisi, but he booked the return flight from Florence, close to Siena. This way, we can check out one more of the Eucharistic miracles from Carlo's exhibit before heading to the airport.

I'm stiff and aching when I climb out of the taxi. My head spins. I'm actually glad to see Father Thomas taking charge of a wheelchair from a smiling Italian priest, who also unlocks the chapel for us. Are they opening up just for me?

Embarrassed but delighted, I try to stay awake as Father Thomas wheels me inside and the Italian priest brings out a fancy glass case containing 223 consecrated Hosts that have somehow remained intact and unrotted for almost three hundred years—something extensive scientific testing has failed to explain.

I try to pray, try to appreciate the moment, but heck, am I tired. Something Carlo's mother said about him comes to mind: he often asked how so many Catholics could stand in long queues to attend rock concerts but couldn't spare five seconds in silence in front of the living God in the tabernacle, to whom we owe our very existence. Um… yeah. I try to concentrate on the miraculous Hosts instead of the thought of getting back into that soft, quiet taxi. Adoration, I read just the other day, brings joy, peace, patience, kindness… what Saint Paul called the fruits of the Holy Spirit. Carlo saw these things growing in his life. Adoration made him "a companion of Jesus."

As I stare at the humble circles of Bread in the glass case, my heart aches inside me. Shaking with the effort, I lever myself out of the wheelchair and sink down on my knees in front of God.

In this moment, I know that I want to be a companion of Jesus too.

Whatever it costs me.

SUNDAY: DAY 8

October 11, 2020

I wake with a dim memory of arriving home very late, of Father Thomas and Dad walking me inside, Father Thomas' reassuring voice echoing in my ears: "He's just very tired. We had a busy day." Of Dad peeling my travel-sweaty clothes off me. And of my own blessed bed, rising up to meet me, my cheek pressing into the soft pillow…

I still feel exhausted, but I'm kind of awake. Arnie's warm weight rests against my back. Reluctantly, I open my eyes, then start so hard it jolts every aching bone in my body and draws a tetchy mew from behind me. "Clare!"

My little sis sits with her chin on the bed, staring into my face.

"Clare, what are you doing?"

"Just… watching you."

"Why?"

"So you don't go away."

"I'm not—" I break off. Bite my lip. Oops, another bruise. "What did Mum and Dad tell you?"

"Dad said you're very sick and you might go away and be gone completely, forever and ever."

I sigh. I want to go back to sleep, but Clare's eyes are filling with tears. "Hey, come here."

She clambers onto the bed, and I wrap my arms around her, holding her close, a bundle of warm life against my diseased body. "It's okay, Clare, all right? Dad didn't explain it well. I am very sick, and, uh, it's not impossible I might die sometime. You understand what that means, right?"

She nods, clinging like a limpet, starting to cry, so I stroke her hair and try to soothe her. *How would Carlo explain this to a six-year-old?* "Shh, listen, Clare. That doesn't mean I'd be gone, okay? I'd still be right here, beside you. You wouldn't be able to see me anymore, and I wouldn't be able to speak to you anymore; but *you* could speak to *me*, and I could pray for you. So, it wouldn't be so very bad as all that, would it? I wouldn't be gone-gone."

"I suppose." Her little voice is muffled by my chest. "But I don't want you to go."

"Me neither," I whisper, my eyelids heavy.

A creak comes from the doorway, as when Mum or Dad is listening to see whether I'm on my computer when I should be in bed, but I'm too sleepy to turn my head and look...

Clare's gone when I wake up again, and the light streaming around the curtains is fading. Arnie's now asleep on my feet. I yawn, stretch, wince, then notice Mum sitting on my couch. "Mum? What are you doing? What time is it?"

She checks her watch. "Almost four."

"In the afternoon? Heck, I've been asleep all day?"

She nods. "Are you hungry?"

"Yeah!" I push back the covers and sit up.

"I can bring you something in bed..."

"What? No, I'm getting up!" I want to go to the six o'clock Mass.

Soon I'm showered and dressed and sitting at the dining room table as everyone tucks into a substantial afternoon tea. Well, I tuck in. Mum can't seem to take her eyes off me as I eat, and Dad keeps shooting me looks too. This is even worse than normal.

"What?" I ask eventually, intercepting Mum's gaze.

She flushes. "Oh, it's just… you haven't stopped smiling since you came home. You're almost… radiant."

My cheeks get hot. "Well, it was such a great trip!" I swallow my last bite and start telling them all about it, finally giving Clare the little Saint Clare rosary bracelet I bought her in the San Damiano gift shop.

Her eyes shining, Clare asks, "She really chased away a whole army?"

"Yes, she did! And she got up out of bed to do it when she was really sick as well."

"Wow!" Clare hugs her bracelet, then hugs me too and dashes out of the room, probably to try it on in front of her little dressing table.

I glance at Dad, who scowled his way through most of my narration. "Dad, aren't you glad I had a good time?"

He just frowns harder. "Of course. But God let you get cancer. How can you still believe He cares about you?"

I take a deep breath, groping for words. The more I've thought about it, the more convinced I am that Father Thomas is right. "Dad, God created me. If He wants to cut and paste me into a different workspace, well, that's up to Him, right? I don't want Him to do it yet—don't get me wrong—but if He does, well, why shouldn't He? So… please don't be mad at Him, okay? I don't want you to be."

Silently, Dad starts gathering up the dirty plates, and I catch a glimpse of the clock in the kitchen. Ten to six. I try to leap to my feet; I achieve a sort of geriatric lurch upright. "Oh no, how am I going to get to Mass in time?" Honestly, I'm not sure I can even walk there, the way I feel.

"Oh Daniel, you don't need to go today," says Mum. "You're so tired!"

"I want to go, Mum! Can't you give me a lift?"

Mum's eyes search my face. "Well... if you're going, I'd like to go too." She avoids my gaze. "I... couldn't quite make myself go this morning. You just... just seemed so tired."

Dad suddenly pulls his car keys from his pocket. "Look, I'll drop you all down there, okay?"

Yes! Impulsively, I step forward and hug him. "Thanks, Dad."

I try not to fume with impatience as Dad stops at another red light. By the time Mum had gotten Clare to put on her shoes, we were running late.

I stare at Dad's profile as we near the church. Both Carlo's parents came back to the faith, right? Heck, why not? "Dad, would you like to come in with us?"

In the front seat, Mum catches her breath, shooting Dad a look. Afraid he's going to yell. Clare raises her car blankie and peeps over it. The fighting must be hurting her too.

Dad says nothing. The lights go green. We're driving down the next street when he finally growls, "Even if I wanted to—which I don't—there won't be a parking space by now."

My heart sinks. He's right. Still, he didn't yell. Mum relaxes again.

Carlo, please pray for a space. Lord, let there be one.

As we pull up outside the church, there's nothing but parked cars as far as the eye can see—not an empty spot in sight. How did people manage to find parking spaces before the virus, when many more people went to Mass? Trying not to sigh audibly, I open the door and ease myself out. I'm so stiff and achy today. I'm trying to keep quiet about my discomfort, though, trying to offer it up, the way Carlo did. When he started to get sick, he immediately offered up all his sufferings for the pope, the Church, and his own entry into heaven.

As I'm about to close the car door, I notice a car pulling out of a parking spot. I lean back inside. "Look, Dad! A space."

"Yeah. Well, you guys go in; you'll be late."

My heart sinking again, I follow Mum, slipping my mask on. Her expression says she doesn't think Dad's going to park. She's probably right. Well, it was worth a try. And he didn't yell.

It's nice to be sitting down, even in a hard pew. I close my eyes and try to remember that feeling of peace, try to prepare myself for Mass. Until someone sits right beside me. My eyes fly open. *Hey, haven't they heard of social dis—* It's Dad!

He's sitting there with his head hunched down on his shoulders like a grumpy turtle—but he's sitting there! I give him a welcoming nod; he grunts.

Father Thomas looks tired when he enters the sanctuary. He would have been doing Masses all morning while I was lying in bed. I'm embarrassed to find myself getting sleepy again by the First Reading. But as the first words sink in, I snap awake.

"On this mountain, the Lord of hosts will prepare for all peoples a banquet of rich food…"

Hang on, is this about heaven? I listen as the reader continues: "On this mountain he will remove the mourning veil covering all peoples, and the shroud enwrapping all nations, he will destroy Death for ever."

I glance at Dad. He sits rigid, a tear running down one cheek. My stomach twists, and I look away quickly. The reader goes on: "The Lord will wipe away the tears from every cheek."

Beside me, Mum takes out a tissue and dabs her eyes. For the first time, like an icy breath through my mind, I wonder: Did the doctor say something extra to Dad while Mum was hugging me and crying over me? Something like "Prepare yourself for the worst"? Is that why they seem so very… I mean, I can't believe Dad said what he said to Clare, even though we won't even get the prognosis until tomorrow.

Oops, I've tuned out the rest of the reading. We're on to the psalm.

"The Lord is my shepherd; there is nothing I shall want…"

Oh boy. That psalm, today? Mum's sobbing now. Maybe the doctor didn't say anything extra. Maybe they're just scared. They're my parents; they feel they should be able to protect me from everything, right? But they can't protect me from this.

"If I should walk in the valley of darkness no evil would I fear. You are there with your crook and your staff; with these you give me comfort."

I grope for Mum's hand, hold it tight.

"In the Lord's own house shall I dwell for ever and ever."

I venture to reach out and give Dad's hand a quick squeeze too. He doesn't react, staring fixedly ahead, so I try to listen to the Second Reading.

"I know how to be poor and I know how to be rich too," the reader begins. That reminds me of Carlo, who lived so simply that he actually argued with his parents when they wanted to buy him a second pair of shoes. He'd save up his money and buy sleeping bags for the homeless. But he was happy to spend money promoting his Eucharistic miracles exhibit. What did he say? Oh yes: "Money is only ragged paper. What counts in life is the nobility of the soul, that is, the way that one loves God and loves one's neighbor."

Ragged paper. Too right. All the money in the world won't

save me, will it?

Money... Oh yeah, I'd almost forgotten. Father Thomas told me that he'd made an online donation to an organization that plants trees to offset carbon emissions, to cover our flights—which I was so pleased to hear, though I admit I'd not even thought about the emissions in all the excitement. I told him I'd give him half the money, but he just told me to make an extra donation, if I cared to. I must do that.

"There is nothing," continues the reader, "I cannot master with the help of the One who gives me strength."

I never believed that before, but Carlo's the proof. Maybe I'm starting to be the proof too. Huh. Weird thought. Am I "mastering" this? Well, I'm trying.

I stay sitting in the pew when Mass is over while Mum takes Clare to light candles and Dad wanders off around the church. Surprise, surprise, I'm feeling shattered, but I try to pray for a few moments in silence, then pull out my phone. I haven't done my novena yet.

To my relief, Carlo's words today are some I'm very familiar with by now: "The Eucharist is my highway to heaven." I don't need to strain my brain over it. I pray the prayer in the meditation: "Give me the grace of a deep fervor for the Eucharist."

Ugh, hang on, I'm getting scatterbrained. I haven't done the opening prayer. I recite it carefully in my head, but when I come to making my request, I hesitate. "For Mum and Dad," I whisper, the way I have been. When I glance over my shoulder, Dad's standing near the door, deep in an earnest—but unusually amiable—conversation with, I quote: "that pip-squeak of a priestly know-it-all," Father Thomas. Father Thomas is so tall and broad, I guess Dad calls him "pip-squeak" just because he's young. But that seems to be going well.

Thanks, Carlo; thanks, Lord.

I add my second request: "Let me live." Then I sit for a long time, flooded with dissatisfaction, feeling Carlo's eyes on me, conscious of Jesus' presence in the tabernacle, wrestling with myself. Finally, I murmur, "Let me live… forever with You."

A wave of stomach-clenching fear immediately washes through me, as if I've just given God permission to kill me or something. I breathe slowly, trying to calm myself. God's going to do whatever He always meant to do. Whatever is best for thick, tunnel-visioned, mortal me. The only thing I can change is my own attitude, right?

All the same, I add under my breath, "Preferably not quite yet, Lord. But… but… well, I suppose it's up to You."

MONDAY: DAY 9—PROGNOSIS DAY

October 12, 2020

Buzz.

Huh? Sleepily, I untangle my arm from the covers and grab my phone. The text is from Razim.

"Pick you up in 10."

Razim's dad has an erratic schedule, but sometimes he takes Razim and me to school on his way to work. Why hasn't Mum woken me?

The hand holding the phone is mottled blue and black with bruises. Oh yeah. It's Prognosis Day. I type: "Sorry, Raz, won't be in school today."

Buzz.

"Why not?"

I hesitate. Finally, I type: "Hospital appointment."

He hasn't replied in the time it takes me to pull the covers up over myself, let my head sink back into the pillow, and close my eyes…

"Daniel?" Mum's voice. Sounding uncertain. I drag my eyes open. "Daniel, Razim's here to see you."

Razim slides past Mum before she can stop him, clearly on a self-appointed mission to find out what's up with me. Mum anxiously looks from him to the lump in the bed that's me.

"It's fine, Mum," I manage. She goes back out, and I push myself up into a sitting position. Only as the duvet slides down do I realize that I'm not wearing a pajama top. I got so tired when I was getting ready for bed last night, I simply didn't bother to put one on. My chest is on display, bruised by every seat I've slept in and every belt I've strapped around me over the last few days.

Razim's jaw drops. "Hey, man, did Marle beat you up?"

"No. Look… I'm sorry I didn't tell you straightaway, but… well, I've got leukemia."

He sinks down on the end of the bed beside Arnie, staring at me. "That's… that's serious, right?"

"Yeah, it's… kind of serious."

His eyes dart nervously from my face to my bruises and back again. "Are you going to… uh…"

"Die?" I surprise myself by how calmly I say the word. "I don't know yet. The doctors are going to give us the prognosis this morning."

He wraps his arms around his own chest, hugging himself, staring at my face. "So… so why do you look so *happy*, man?"

I shrug and shove my fingers through my hair, which I may not have for much longer. "It's been a heck of a week. You'll never guess where I was on Saturday!"

His eyes flick over me. "Hospital?"

"Italy!"

"*Italy*? I thought you were sick, man!"

"I am! But that's why I got to go, would you believe?"

Can I talk to Raz about faith stuff? For a moment, I hesitate. His family isn't religious at all, just culturally Muslim. Then I remember how Carlo got confirmed at eleven and immediately became an evangelist. How he chatted to all sorts of different people on the way to school each day, making friends with loads of immigrants—Hindus, Muslims, Buddhists—everyone. He was even the godfather when one of them got baptized! When he died, they all turned up to pay their respects, which shocked the socks off his parents, who didn't know anything about them.

I grab the prayer card Father Thomas gave me, what feels like a hundred years ago, from where Mum placed it on the bedside table when she took my clothes to wash. "Look! This guy's name is Carlo. He's the reason I got to go to Assisi."

Hesitantly at first, but then gathering confidence, I start to tell him about Carlo and the beatification trip. Once I've started talking, I can't stop. Raz sits, eyes wide, shoulders tense, as if he can't decide whether he wants to back away or inch closer.

"Raz, have you heard that Steve Jobs quote? Carlo loved it—and totally lived it. Let me try and remember..." I screw my face up, and the words come; I've read them often this week. "Your time is limited, so do not waste it living someone else's life... Being the richest man in the cemetery doesn't matter to me.... Going to bed at night saying we've done something wonderful—that's what matters to me."

I stop talking only when Mum opens the door to inform us that Razim's dad has been honking outside for twenty minutes, and don't we realize Razim is going to be dreadfully late for school?

"Hey, good luck today, man." Raz reaches out to give me a slap on the back, then converts it to a gentle fist bump.

"Thanks."

Out he goes, throwing one last concerned, wide-eyed look back at me. Is he going to tell everyone I've turned into some sort of Jesus freak? I'm surprised to find how little I care.

I probably won't be in school much for the next little while, anyway.

Besides, I don't want to be a photocopy anymore.

When Mum wakes me again to get ready for the appointment—I dozed straight off after Raz left—I realize I haven't done my novena yet. I grab my phone quickly.

Oh boy. It would be *this* quote today. "I am happy to die because I have lived my life without wasting a minute on those things which do not please God." And the prayer: "Give me that grace of graces—perseverance to the end and a saintly death."

Despite my lingering euphoria from Saturday—and from what happened with Dad last night—I'm getting kind of scared again, reading that, this morning of all mornings.

Then I remember what Father Thomas said. *We all die.* So, I guess this prayer is important for everyone. And it's important for me, no matter what the prognosis.

I finish day 9 of the novena, then realize I've forgotten the opening prayer again. I want to make the same—revised—request as last night, but it sticks in my throat, which feels tight with dread.

I keep my eyes closed and breathe slowly and deeply, trying to find the peace I bottled in Assisi. I don't entirely stop feeling tense and on edge, but eventually I hear more of Carlo's words, whispering through my mind: *Our aim has to be the Infinite and not the finite. The Infinite is our homeland. We have always been expected in heaven.*

He died so peacefully, so joyfully. So *generously.* Because he had his priorities right. Because he knew where his true home was. And he's obviously there, in heaven. There was at least one confirmed, medically investigated miracle prior to the beatification. And all sorts of other things. He promised his parents signs—*signs*, not *a* sign—that he was with God, and his mother gave birth to twins exactly four years after he died, to the day, when she was forty-four, which is pretty old to have babies, apparently. Carlo's parents were sure the twins were the promised signs.

And there was a young priest in Costa Rica who dreamed three times about a smiling teenage boy who wanted to meet all the priest's friends so he could help them love God more. Later in the month the priest saw—for the very first time—a photo of Carlo and recognized him at once from his dream! And what Carlo's done for me this week, with his prayers and encouragement… and for Mum and Dad… yeah, he's reached our true home, all right.

I'm "expected" there too. Maybe I'll be joining him soon. Maybe not for a while. Maybe not for a long time. But if that really is where I want to be one day, I need to focus on that, whatever the doctor says today. I don't want to let fear choke the new life that's blooming inside me. I refuse to be afraid of something as wonderful as… as being with God.

Eyes still closed, I whisper my request. "For Mum and Dad. And let me live forever with You. When You're ready for me. Amen."

"Daniel?" A nurse comes into the waiting room. "The consultant will see you now. Just make your way through."

Mum leaps to her feet, and I get up too. Dad's already standing, pacing the room. We walk out into the corridor and pause outside the door opposite. Dad reaches out and grips Mum's hand tightly. She gulps a breath that's half a sob.

I turn and hug her as tightly as I dare—or maybe slightly tighter. What's a few more bruises at this stage? "It's okay, Mum. It's going to be okay. You understand that, right? Whatever happens, everything will be fine."

Her eyes smile at me over her mask when I let her go again, a watery smile. "Ah, Daniel, look at you. Quite the man now. I can't believe how much you've grown up this last week."

I shrug, embarrassed. "I'll always be your little boy, right?"

She hugs me again, tight. When she finally lets me go, I glance at Dad. "Shall we go in?"

He nods, but no one moves. I look at the door and picture Carlo standing beside me. Yeah, it doesn't matter what they say in there. I've got a friend who's helping me sort out my priorities. And everything's going to be okay. Either way.

I take a deep breath, square my shoulders, open the door—and take the next step on my journey home.

PRAYER TO SAINT CARLO ACUTIS

Carlo, smile of Heaven
for this wounded and peaceless world,
we praise God
for your simple, joyful, and holy life.
You accepted with trust
to be stripped of your youth
to dedicate yourself in Heaven,
with Jesus and Mary,
to a mission of boundless love.

Resting with your mortal body
where Francis of Assisi
stripped himself of every earthly good,
you cry out with him to the world that
Jesus is all our joy.

Young man, full of dreams,
attracted by nature, by sports, by the Internet,
but even more enraptured by the miracle
of Jesus truly present in the Sacred Host,
help us to believe that He is there alive and real,
the mystical "highway" that leads to Heaven,
and teach us to contemplate Him with Mary,
in the mysteries of the Holy Rosary.
Explain to us, Carlo, that, beyond every fashion,
only Jesus, by uniting ourselves to Him,
makes us "originals and not photocopies,"
truly free.

Grant us to know how to meet Him
in every creature, but especially in the poor,
so that humanity may be more just and fraternal,
rich in beauty and hope,
to the glory of the Father, the Son,
and the Holy Spirit.
Amen.

Our Father, Hail Mary, Glory Be

Imprimatur + Domenico Sorrentino
Archbishop of Assisi
Nocera Umbra, Gualdo Tadino, Foligno

NOVENA TO SAINT CARLO ACUTIS

Opening Prayer

Most Holy Trinity, Father, Son, and Holy Spirit, I thank You for all the grace and favors with which you enriched the soul of Saint Carlo Acutis during his fifteen years on this earth. Through the merits of this Angel of Youth, grant me the grace which I earnestly seek.
(*Ask the grace which you seek.*)

Day 1: "Not me, but God."

Saint Carlo Acutis, you who made your life a continual renunciation and setting aside of unimportant things, give me the grace to seek heavenly things and despise that which is transient. Amen.

Pray five Our Fathers, five Hail Marys, and five Glory Bes to give thanks to God for the grace granted to Carlo in the fifteen years of his earthly life.

Day 2: "Always to be united with Jesus—that is my life's program."

Saint Carlo Acutis, you who have lived in the heart of Jesus, give me the grace to apply Jesus' plan of love to everything. Amen.

Pray five Our Fathers, five Hail Marys, and five Glory Bes to give thanks to God for the grace granted to Carlo in the fifteen years of his earthly life.

Day 3: "Continuously ask your guardian angel for help. Your guardian angel has to become your best friend."

Saint Carlo Acutis, you who saw the company of holy angels while you were already in this world, give me the grace to live righteously, as my guardian angel desires. Amen.

Pray five Our Fathers, five Hail Marys, and five Glory Bes to give thanks to God for the grace granted to Carlo in the fifteen years of his earthly life.

Day 4: "Our soul is like a hot-air balloon. If by chance there is a mortal sin, the soul falls to the ground. Confession is like the fire underneath the balloon enabling the soul to rise again.... It is important to go to confession often."

Saint Carlo Acutis, you who have lived this sacrament of reconciliation so well, give me the grace constantly to seek confession and the grace of a deep contrition. Amen.

Pray five Our Fathers, five Hail Marys, and five Glory Bes to give thanks to God for the grace granted to Carlo in the fifteen years of his earthly life.

Day 5: "Sadness is looking at ourselves; happiness is looking toward God."

Saint Carlo Acutis, you who have never looked away from your great love, Jesus, give me the grace also to live with this happiness in this world. Amen.

Pray five Our Fathers, five Hail Marys, and five Glory Bes to give thanks to God for the grace granted to Carlo in the fifteen years of his earthly life.

Day 6: "The only thing we have to ask God for, in prayer, is the desire to be holy."

Saint Carlo Acutis, you who have always asked God for what is essential, give me the grace of a deep desire for heaven. Amen.

Pray five Our Fathers, five Hail Marys, and five Glory Bes to give thanks to God for the grace granted to Carlo in the fifteen years of his earthly life.

Day 7: "The Virgin Mary is the only Woman in my life."

Saint Carlo Acutis, you who loved the Virgin Mary above all women, give me the grace to respond to her kind and good love. Amen.

Pray five Our Fathers, five Hail Marys, and five Glory Bes to give thanks to God for the grace granted to Carlo in the fifteen years of his earthly life.

Day 8: "The Eucharist is my highway to heaven."

Saint Carlo Acutis, you who have always looked for your hidden Jesus in the tabernacle, give me the grace of a deep fervor for the Eucharist. Amen.

Pray five Our Fathers, five Hail Marys, and five Glory Bes to give thanks to God for the grace granted to Carlo in the fifteen years of his earthly life.

Day 9: "I am happy to die because I have lived my life without wasting a minute on those things which do not please God."

Saint Carlo Acutis, give me that grace of graces—perseverance to the end and a saintly death. Amen.

Pray five Our Fathers, five Hail Marys, and five Glory Bes to give thanks to God for the grace granted to Carlo in the fifteen years of his earthly life.

Final Prayer

Almighty God, Father of Mercy, you have raised Saint Carlo Acutis to the glory of the altars, so that through him You will be even more glorified. Through his merit, give me the grace that I so ardently desire. Amen.[1]

Carlo's feast day is October 12.

Imprimatur + Dom Janusz Marian Danecki, O.F.M.Conv., Auxiliary Bishop of the Diocese of Campo Grande, Brazil

1. This prayer has been updated since Carlo Acutis was declared a saint on September 7, 2025

DISCUSSION QUESTIONS

1. *Daniel and Carlo received very similar medical diagnoses, but there is quite a difference in their reactions.*
   – Whose response do you identify more with?
   – Is that how you think you might respond?
   – Why?
   – Would you prefer to respond differently?

2. *Daniel's mother turns to God in the face of this challenge, but his father rejects God.*
   – Why do you think they react in such different ways?
   – Whose reaction do you identify more with?
   – Why?

3. *Carlo loved playing video games but strictly limited how long he played them in order to make time for things like working in the homeless shelter, prayer, and working on his Eucharistic miracles project.*
   – Do you ever struggle to find time for prayer, charitable work, or other faith activities?
   – Is there something in your life that, although harmless or even beneficial when used properly, is taking up too much of your time?
   – Could you easily scale back this activity?
   – If not, why not? (Addictions come in many shapes and forms and always draw us away from God.)

4. *Carlo talked openly about his Catholic faith and morality at school and among his friends. Under his influence, and that of the Holy Spirit, Daniel gains the courage to do the same.*
   – Do you speak openly about such things?
   – Why or why not?
   – Why does it matter?

5. *Father Thomas uses the metaphor of an artist's pot to explain to Daniel that he is a created thing, God's creation.*
   – What do you think of this metaphor?
   – Does it work for you?
   – Why or why not?
   – Can you think of a better one?

6. *Daniel learns something very important during the course of the story, and it is for this reason that the story ends just before he receives his prognosis instead of just after.*
   – What is it that Daniel learns?
   – Why would learning his prognosis undercut this?

MORE INFORMATION

Biographies

– Antonia Salzano Acutis with Paolo Rodari, *My Son Carlo: Carlo Acutis through the Eyes of His Mother* (Huntington, IN: Our Sunday Visitor, 2023)

– Courtney Mares, *Blessed Carlo Acutis: A Saint in Sneakers* (San Francisco: Ignatius, 2023).

– Francesco Occhetta, *Carlo Acutis, the Servant of God: Life beyond the Border* (Gorle, Italy: Velar, 2018).

Spirituality

– Anthony Figueiredo, *Blessed Carlo Acutis: 5 Steps to Being a Saint* (London: Catholic Truth Society, 2021)

– Ephrem Kunnappally, *Highway to Heaven: A Spiritual Journey through the Life of Blessed Carlo Acutis* (Parayanchery, Kerala, India: Atma Books / Pavanatma, 2020).

Online Resources

– Official website of the Carlo Acutis Association: www.carloacutis.com/en/association.

– Videos, prayers, and other information: https://carloacutis-en.org/.

– Links to Carlo's exhibitions: http://www.carloacutis.com/.

ACKNOWLEDGMENTS

I'd like to thank Theoni Bell, Karina Fabian, Melinda Harrington, Jason C. Miller, and Susan Peek for all their excellent editorial help.

Thanks to my parents for all their support, and to my mother for her honest critiques.

Big thanks to Colleen Angela, for the fantastic cover artwork on the original edition. Many thanks also to the team at Magnificat and Ignatius for their work on this new edition.

And I cannot forget Saint Carlo Acutis, the patron of this book—and last but the opposite of least, the Holy Spirit, who is responsible for it all.

ABOUT THE AUTHOR

Corinna Turner has been writing since she was fourteen and likes strong protagonists with plenty of integrity. Although she spends as much time as possible writing, she cannot keep up with the flow of ideas, for which she offers thanks—and occasional grumbles!—to the Holy Spirit. She is the author of over thirty books, including the Carnegie Medal–nominated I Am Margaret series, and her work has been translated into four languages. She was awarded the Saint Katherine Drexel Award in 2022.

She is a lay Dominican with a master's in English from Oxford University and lives in the United Kingdom. She is a member of a number of organizations, including the Society of Authors, Catholic Teen Books, Catholic Reads, the Angelic Warfare Confraternity, and the Sodality of the Blessed Sacrament. She used to have a giant African land snail, Peter, with a six-and-a-half-inch shell, but now makes do with a cactus and a campervan.

First published 2020, online only, by Unseen Books USA, an imprint of Zephyr publishing

Published 2024 by Magnificat, New York • Ignatius Press, San Francisco

ISBN Magnificat 978-1-63967-094-9 • ISBN Ignatius Press 978-1-62164-717-1
E-book ISBN: 978-1-63967-095-6